Why, Zaida?

Why, Zaida?

by

ALVIN ABRAM

Illustrations by

Judy Nora Willemsma

Design, typesetting and layout by

Dennis Rowe

AMA*Graphics* Incorporated
Toronto, Ontario, Canada

Published Stories

Tabloids:

CANADIAN JEWISH NEWS:

Who's There? A Yid. (1997)
The Cloth Coat (1998)
What If… (1999)

THE BAYVIEW POST:

The Cloth Coat (1999)

Non-fiction:

THE LIGHT AFTER THE DARK (1998):

- *An Eye For An Eye [Zalman Katz]*
- *The Promise [Michael Kutz]*
- *We Will Meet Again [Moishe Perlmutter]*
- *I Have a Mission [Dubi Arie]*
- *I Knew My Enemy [Michael Rosenberg]*
- *Don't Worry: It Will Be Good [Faigie Libman and Batia Malamud]*

Fiction:

WORDSCAPE 4: MYSTERY & SUSPENSE 1997 (467 pages)
Anthology book published by Metropolitan Toronto Authors Association

- *Ta-Ta-T-A-Ta*
- *Growing Old*
- *A Story in Two Words*

WORDSCAPE 5: MYSTERY & SUSPENSE 1998 (440 pages)
Anthology book published by Metropolitan Toronto Authors Association

- *Late Again Harry*

WORDSCAPE 6: MYSTERY & SUSPENSE 1999 (440 pages)

- *The Credit Card Caper*

WINNERS CIRCLE: 1998 (158 pages)
Fifteen stories selected by merit
Metropolitan Toronto Authors Association

- *The Baker*

Poetry:

- *I'm A Jew (Abbeyfield: 1997)*
- *Love With Respect (Anthology: 1997)*
- *The Chanukah Lamp (Canadian Jewish News: 1998)*

Why, Zaida?
זיידה פרוואס?

To my granddaughter
Ally Rayna Brown

Your smile and personality
make the pain go away.

– Zaida Alvin

Published by AMA*Graphics* Incorporated
1111 Finch Avenue West, Unit 19, Toronto, Ontario M3J 2E5 Canada
www.amagraphics.com

Watercolour illustrations by Judy Nora Willemsma
Design, typesetting and layout by Dennis Rowe
Film by Greater Graphics (Toronto)
Lithography by Press Partners (Toronto)

Printed and bound in Canada

Canadian Cataloguing in Publication Data

Alvin Abram, 1936-
Why, Zaida?

ISBN 0-9692398-2-3

1. Holocaust, Jewish (1939-1945) – Juvenile fiction. I. Willemsma, Judy. II. Title.

PS8551.B49W49 2000 jC813'.6 C00-930729-X
PZ7.A1688Wh 2000

INTRODUCTION

Why? What a word! When spoken by a grieving adult, it's a wail of pain. When asked by the young and innocent, it's a word filled with curiosity. So many times I have heard the pain in a Holocaust survivor's voice as they related hesitantly, softly, reluctantly, their story. "*Why?*" they asked themselves, could they not find an answer to satisfy the anguish they felt. And then, after a pause to reflect, they would ask, "*Why, me?*"

Is there an answer? Can there ever be an answer? I don't believe so, but there can be closure. I've seen it. For more than fifty years, historians have pounded into the minds of Holocaust victims that they lived while millions died. They were left with a legacy of guilt and carried it wherever they went.

The children bore their parents' guilt by witnessing their grief. They saw the burden and were unable to lift it. Some could not cope with their parents' world and became estranged; damaged by their association.

The victims, now called survivors, asked of what value was in their survival? And the answer, the why – became the grandchild – a progeny born only because they did survive. Pure and untouched, a vessel filled each day with universal knowledge and marvellous experiences, born of a new generation. Love is the lining that coats the vessel and love will be the balm that heals.

"*Why, Zaida did you survive?*" So you my grandchild can change the world to be a better place.

A. Abram.

An old man and a young boy sat close together beside a stream. The similarity of their features – the contour of the head, the shape of the chin and nose – showed they were related. Neither spoke as they listened to the rushing water, the birds, the squirrels, the breeze and their thoughts.

The old man had passed his seventieth birthday and now his life revolved around his son and grandson. He loved them both. They were his hold on the world he had built after surviving the war and the Holocaust. But today he was troubled. His son had told him his grandson was asking questions – ones the old man would rather not answer.

The clear stream bumped its way down the slight incline, churning into white froth where it struck the scattered partially submerged rocks. Multicoloured leaves floated along the surface, moulding themselves to the ups and downs of the current. The little boy looked up at his grandfather and said, *"Zaida, birds have fathers and mothers, don't they?"*

The old man had just flipped a pebble into the stream. *"Yes,"* he said softly.

A squirrel scampered in front of them, an acorn in its mouth. The squirrel stopped, his teeth grinding away at the morsel.

"Zaida, squirrels have fathers and mothers too, don't they?"

The old man looked solemnly at the young boy. *"Yes, of course they do."*

The little boy frowned. *"Then how come you never had a father or a mother?"*

"That's not true. Why are you asking?"

"I never saw them. There are no pictures of them. Nobody talks about them. That's why."

The old man gazed at a floating branch as it bobbed and dipped over each wave until its progress, halted by two rocks was trapped as water ran over and around it.

"It's hard to explain," he whispered.

"Why, Zaida? What's so hard?"

The old man continued to stare at the trapped stick. I'm like the stick, he thought. Trapped in my head are images of the past and I can't find the key to open the door. What do I tell him? I was his age when it all happened and I don't understand why I had to suffer such pain.

Upsetting the delicate balance, the changing current released the stick and it floated out of sight. The old man stared at the water rushing freely between the two rocks.

"Zaida?"

He looked down at his grandson, choking back his feelings before replying.

"They…they died when I was very young."

"Why?"

"Because."

"Daddy said 'because' is not an answer. It's an excuse."

The old man grinned. *"I know. I told him that."*

"Why did they die? Were they sick?"

"No, they weren't sick." He looked about, desperately trying to find the right words to answer his grandson.

A robin landed on the ground, jabbed its beak into the grass and came up with a worm, then flew into the trees.

"Did you see what the robin did?" the old man asked.

The boy nodded.

"Robins put into their mouths only what they can eat. Many years ago, a bad man started eating. He ate people who were ill and many cheered. Next he ate people who caused problems and some cheered that too. Then he ate good people. Those who had cheered were confused. Finally he ate everyone and no one was left to disagree."

"Is that what happened to your mother and father?"

"Yes, and many others. Everyone thought the bad man was either mad or a genius. Those who thought him mad ignored him, and those who thought he was a genius followed him. He ate and ate, and others ate with him and everything they ate, they destroyed."

"Why was he so hungry?"

"He lived with hate and jealousy in his heart. Each desire gnawed at him until all he saw was ugliness. There was no beauty in his life."

The little boy pondered the old man's words, a frown across his brow.

Just then the squirrel in front of them stopped eating and sat on its haunches. Its head turned in all directions in quick, jerky motions. The old man touched the young boy on the shoulder.

"Watch," he said.

A dog had appeared just over a rise and barrelled down toward the squirrel, barking and yelping. The squirrel dropped the partially eaten acorn, leaped toward the nearest tree and scampered up the trunk. Barking and wagging its tail, the dog jumped against the trunk. Accepting he had lost his prey, he ran away to look for his next adventure.

The young boy laughed.

"The bad man picked on the weak. He did it to draw attention to himself. He jumped and barked, frightening those unable to help themselves. The dog was having fun, but the squirrel didn't know it. It was frightened."

The little boy dropped his head to his chest.

"I'm sorry, Zaida. I laughed. I thought it was funny. I wasn't thinking of the squirrel."

"I know. It was the same when the bad man made fun of the weak. Others joined him. It wasn't funny for those who were his victims."

"What's a victim?" The little boy gazed up at the old man and noticed a tear on his cheek.

"Are you crying, Zaida?"

The old man shook his head and smiled. *"I was remembering."*

"Remembering what?"

"My mother and father. They were victims. They didn't understand what the bad man was doing. They couldn't believe the stories they heard. One day they found out the truth."

"Daddy said the truth never hurts. It's when you don't tell the truth that it hurts."

"Yes, lies hurt…but the truth can also hurt.

One day, bad men came for my father and took him to a bad place. Then my mother understood the truth and gave me to a family to keep me safe. Later they came for my mother."

"What happened to the bad man? Did he get punished?"

"I want you to look at the water and wait for a leaf to float down," the old man said.

They stared at the rushing stream in silence. The old man pointed.

"There – do you see it coming?"

"Yes! Yes!" The little boy cried excitedly.

"Watch what happens when it reaches the two rocks in front of us. Don't lose sight of it."

"I won't."

The leaf slapped the rock and was momentarily pasted against its surface, but the continuous rush of water under it, pried it loose and it floated uncontrollably out of sight.

"For a little while, it looked like the bad man might succeed, but the good people gained strength and chipped away until he could no longer withstand them. He was stopped, but it was too late for so many."

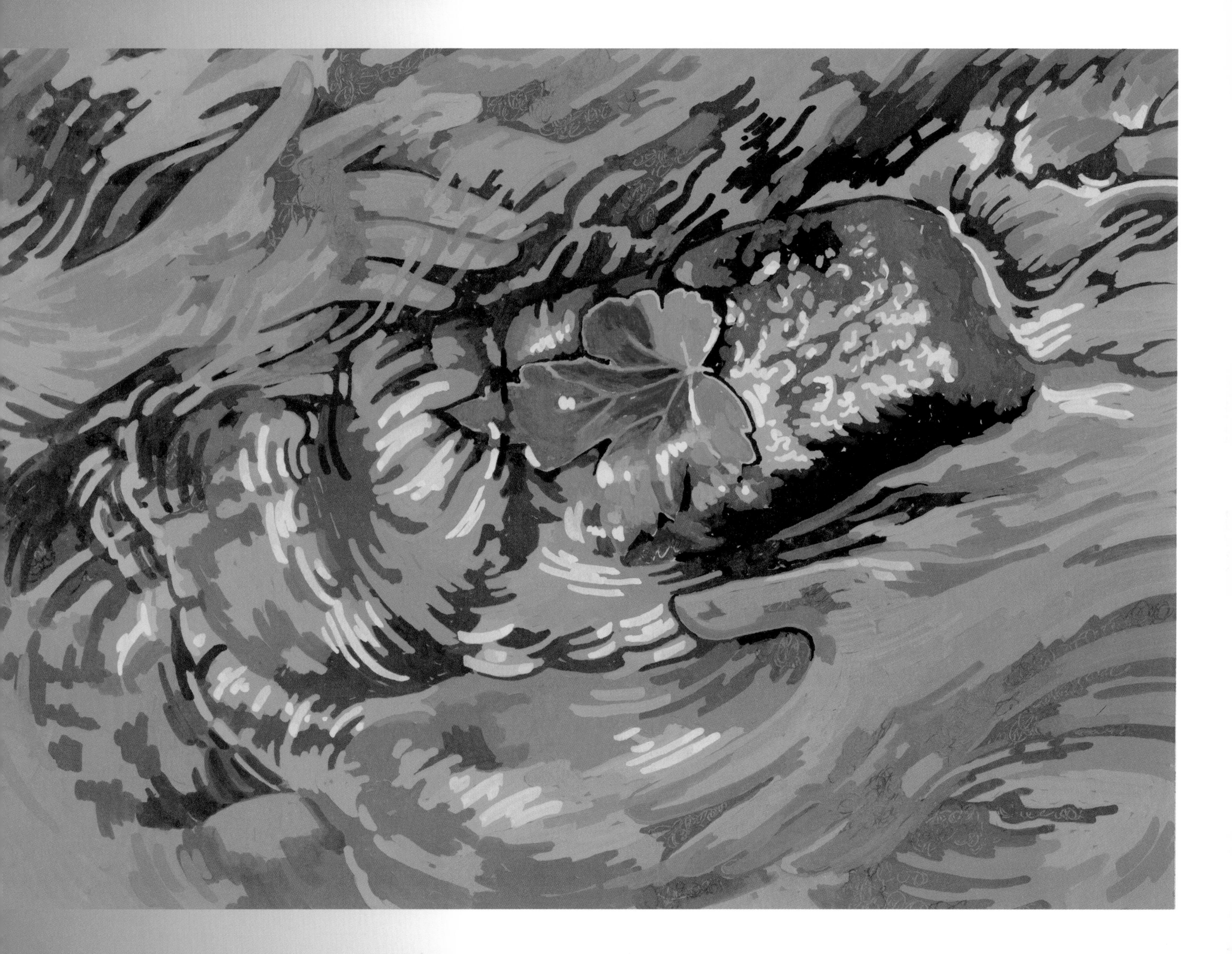

"Is that man still here?" the grandson asked.

The old man looked about before answering. *"Do you see the grass?"*

The young boy smiled, *"Yes, Zaida. It's everywhere."*

"Grass grows all over the world. Among the grass, weeds grow. Sometimes in clumps and sometimes alone. Weeds are bad. They take instead of giving to the soil. That bad man is gone, but others spring up all over the world and they cause ugliness wherever they appear."

"Why don't people stop them?"

"Some try, but most are afraid. They hope, if they don't get involved, maybe they'll be left alone. But another weed grows beside the first and another, until there is a clump, and by then the good grass has been eaten and is gone."

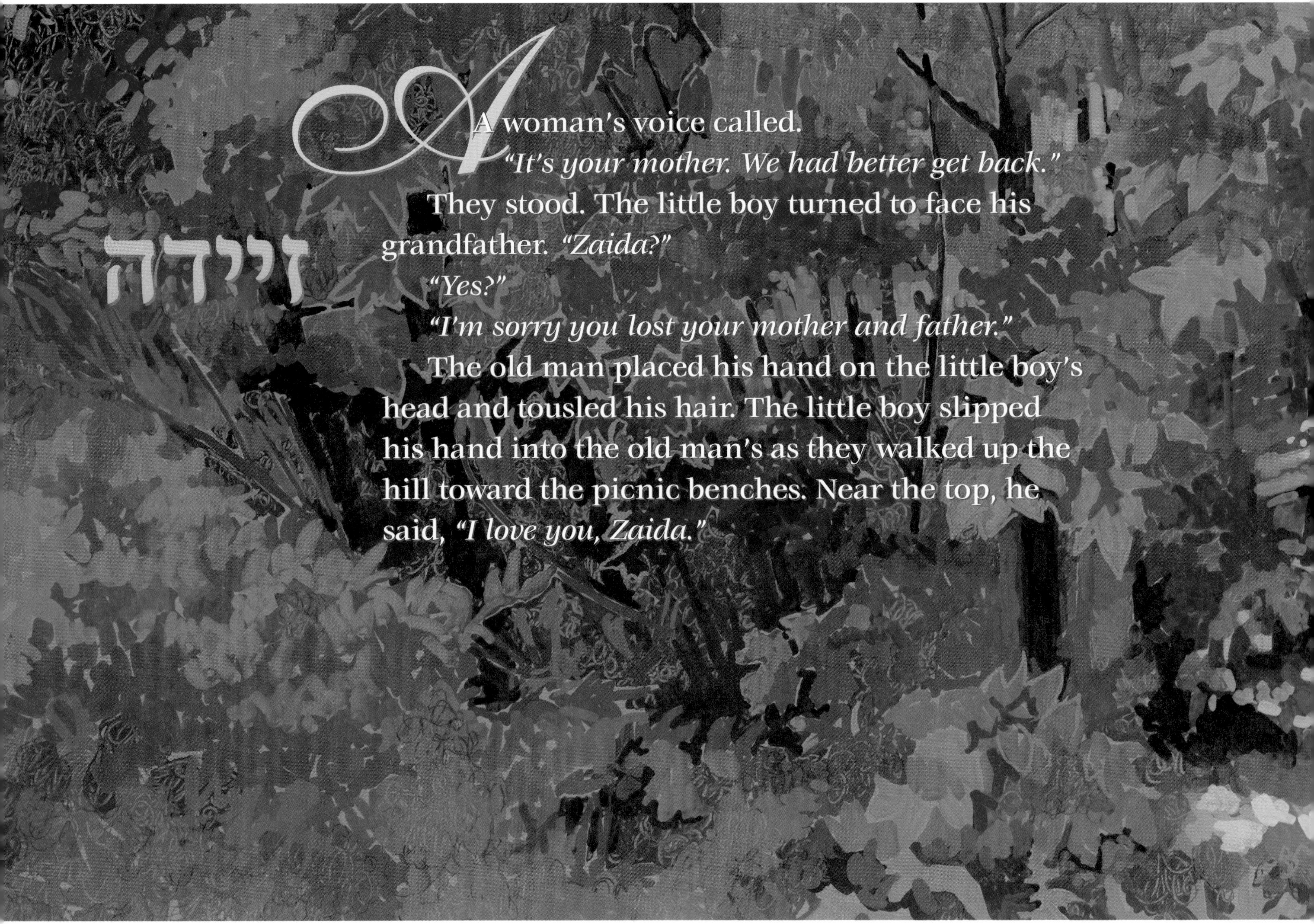

זיידה

A woman's voice called.

"It's your mother. We had better get back."

They stood. The little boy turned to face his grandfather. *"Zaida?"*

"Yes?"

"I'm sorry you lost your mother and father."

The old man placed his hand on the little boy's head and tousled his hair. The little boy slipped his hand into the old man's as they walked up the hill toward the picnic benches. Near the top, he said, *"I love you, Zaida."*

The squirrel came down from the tree and scampered around until it found the partially nibbled acorn. It froze momentarily when it heard the yapping of the dog, but realized it was not in immediate danger and continued to chip away at its lunch. The stream danced down the slight incline and multicoloured leaves bounced along its surface. Everything was as it was before.

Or was it?

זיידה This is a picture of the Yiddish characters for “Zaida,” which means “Grandfather” in English

זיידה פרוואס? This is a picture of the Yiddish characters for “Why, Zaida?”

זיידה פרוואס? These are the Yiddish characters which mean “Why, Zaida?”

Questions asked children 9-11:

1. *What was Zaida's first reaction when the little boy asked him about his parents?*
2. *Why did Zaida react this way?*
3. *Who was Zaida referring to when he talked about “the bad man?”*
4. *Why didn't he use “the bad man's” real name?*
5. *Why did Zaida feel he was like the stick caught in the stream?*
6. *What did Zaida mean when he said that he was old and still didn't understand how something like this could have taken place?*
7. *Instead of explaining the Holocaust in exact terms, he used the analogy of “eating.” Did you like the way he explained the Holocaust?*
8. *How would you have explained it?*
9. *Did the little boy understand?*
10. *The story ends, “Everything was as it was before. Or was it?” What had changed?*

Name: ______________________________ Age: ____________________